STARS OF SPORTS

AUSTON MATTHEWS

HOCKEY DYNAMO

by Shane Frederick

CAPSTONE PRESS
a capstone imprint

Stars of Sports is published by
Capstone Press, an imprint of Capstone
1710 Roe Crest Drive, North Mankato, Minnesota 56003
www.capstonepub.com

**Library of Congress Cataloging-in-Publication Data is available
on the Library of Congress website.**
978-1-5435-9172-9 (library binding)
978-1-5435-9186-6 (eBook PDF)

Summary: Auston Matthews felt at home on the ice as soon as he stepped onto a
rink as a kid. Soon hockey scouts watched him closely as he broke records in the
youth hockey league. After signing with the Toronto Maple Leafs, he made an
immediate impact by being the first player in the modern era to score four goals in
his National Hockey League debut. Learn about the rise of a three-time NHL All-
Star in this exciting, fast-paced biography.

Editorial Credits
Editor: Hank Musolf; Designer: Ashlee Suker; Media Researcher: Eric Gohl;
Production Specialist: Laura Manthe

Image Credits
Associated Press: Paul Connors, 11; Getty Images: Bruce Bennett, 13, Kevin Sousa,
28; Newscom: Icon Sportswire/John Crouch, 23, Icon Sportswire/Wayne Szeto/
John Crouch, 16, Reuters/Jeff Topping, 8, USA Today Sports/Dan Hamilton, 26,
USA Today Sports/Jerry Lai, 25, USA Today Sports/Marc DesRosiers, 5, 7, USA
Today Sports/Matt Kartozian, 24, USA Today Sports/Tom Szczerbowski, cover,
ZUMA Press/Aleksander Kulebyakin, 18, ZUMA Press/Freshfocus/Andy Mueller,
15, ZUMA Press/Freshfocus/Steffen Schmidt, 21, ZUMA Press/Lucas Oleniuk, 27,
ZUMA Press/Nicola Pitaro, 19; Shutterstock: Adam Vilimek, 1

All internet sites appearing in back matter were available and accurate when this
book was sent to press.

Direct Quotations
Pages 22, from June 24, 2016, CBC article "NHL Draft: Toronto Maple Leafs pick
Auston Matthews 1st overall", https://www.cbc.ca

Printed in the United States of America.
PA99

TABLE OF CONTENTS

Glossary terms are **BOLD** on first use.

A STAR IS BORN

The first game for any National Hockey League (NHL) player is special. The first time Auston Matthews played for the Toronto Maple Leafs was no different. It was a night he would never forget.

It was opening night of the 2016 NHL season. The Maple Leafs were playing against the Ottawa Senators. All eyes were on 19-year-old Matthews. Three months earlier, he was the number one overall pick in the draft. Matthews was lucky enough to score a goal in the first period of his first NHL game. Standing in front of the net, he took a pass from teammate Zach Hyman and fired the puck past the goaltender. But Matthews was just getting started. He scored three more times!

Matthews skates in his first NHL game in 2016. 〉〉〉

NHL players rarely score four goals in their first game. The crowd cheered after every goal. Many of them were fans of the visiting team, the Maple Leafs. But fans of the home team celebrated too. They knew they were seeing the birth of a superstar.

After Matthews netted his third goal for a **hat trick**, TV cameras spotted his parents in the arena. They were happy for their 19-year-old son. Matthews had taken a long journey to get to the NHL.

FACT

Matthews's four-goal first game is a modern-era NHL record. The modern era began in 1943. In 1917, Joe Malone of the Montreal Canadiens and Harry Hyland of the Montreal Wanderers each scored five goals in their NHL debut.

Matthews celebrated with his teammates after his first NHL goal. 〉〉〉

CHAPTER ONE
ARIZONA ICE

Auston Matthews is a **unique** hockey player. He wasn't raised in a place where hockey is played by a lot of people. He grew up in Arizona. Arizona is a state known for being hot and having dry deserts, not for frozen lakes or hockey rinks.

Matthews was born on September 17, 1997, in California. When he was very young, his family moved to Scottsdale, Arizona, near the state capital of Phoenix. A year before Matthews was born, an NHL team moved to Arizona from Canada. The team was called the Coyotes. Many kids began to skate and become hockey players in Arizona after that. Matthews was one of them.

《《《 The Phoenix Coyotes in 1999

HOCKEY FAVORITES

Matthews went to his first Coyotes game with his dad and his uncle when he was 2 years old. He soon fell in love with hockey. Matthews's favorite Coyotes players were Shane Doan and Daniel Briere.

Matthews began playing hockey when he was 5 years old. His parents didn't know much about the sport, but they could see that their son had a passion for the game. Hockey can be an expensive sport, so Matthews's mother worked two jobs to help her son follow his dreams.

In 2006, 8-year-old Matthews was in the arena when Washington Capitals star Alexander Ovechkin scored "The Goal." It was one of the most amazing hockey plays of all-time. Ovechkin put the puck in the net with a backhanded shot over his head after falling to the ice. Matthews was starting to score some amazing goals of his own. But he didn't know that one day he'd play in games against Doan and Ovechkin.

〉〉〉 Alex Ovechkin scored "The Goal" on January 16, 2006.

FACT

Alexander Ovechkin has had a legendary NHL career. In March 2019, he broke the record for the most 45-goal seasons. It was the 10th season he had scored 45 goals or more.

CHAPTER TWO

AUSTON ON THE RISE

Matthews was born into an athletic family. His dad, Brian, played baseball in college. Matthews's great-uncle, Wes Matthews, played professional football for the Miami Dolphins. Brian believed baseball was Matthews's best sport. Matthews liked baseball, but he thought there was too much standing around. Matthews craved the fast-paced action of hockey.

Although there weren't many rinks around Arizona yet, Matthews played hockey whenever he had the chance. Sometimes he skated against older players, but he fit right in.

Matthews celebrated with his parents after being drafted to the Toronto Maple Leafs. 〉〉〉

People who watched young Matthews were impressed by his puck handling, shooting, and skating. But they were most amazed by how hard Matthews worked to improve his skills.

TRAVELS BEGIN

Matthews worked with a special coach to become a better skater. The coach was from a country in Europe called Ukraine. He later became the national coach for Mexico.

Matthews joined a program called the Arizona Bobcats. The Bobcats played games and tournaments all around North America. When Matthews played for the Bobcats' Under-16 team, he scored 55 goals and had 45 **assists** for 100 points in 48 games. Coaches and scouts noticed Matthews's impressive **statistics**.

FACT

Before moving to Arizona, the Coyotes were the Winnipeg Jets. Winnipeg, a city in Canada, was without a team for 15 years. In 2011, the Atlanta Thrashers moved there, and the Jets were reborn.

〉〉〉 Matthews speeds ahead during a 2015 game.

CHAPTER THREE
LEAVING HOME

Matthews tried out for the United States' national team when he was 16. The team looks for possible rising stars and trains them. Matthews earned a spot. The coach, Don Granato, told Matthews's dad that his son's life was about to change. Matthews had to move to Michigan to be part of the program. It was his first time living away from home.

Things didn't start off well. In his second game, Matthews suffered a broken leg and had to have surgery. He missed three months of the season. When Matthews returned to the ice, though, he played as if he had missed no time at all. He averaged more than one point per game.

《《《 Matthews impressed the USA junior team's coaches.

UNDER-18 MVP

The next season, Matthews played for the Under-18 national team. He played against the best junior and college teams in the United States and other teams from around the world. Matthews often was the best player on the ice. In 60 games, Matthews broke two team records. He had scored 55 goals and had 117 points. No one had scored that much over 60 games. Those records were set nine years earlier by Patrick Kane. Kane went on to become a star player for the Chicago Blackhawks.

〉〉〉 Matthews clashes with Thomas Chabot in a World Junior Championship game against Canada in 2015.

Matthews also played in two Under-18 World Championships in 2014 and 2015. He led Team USA to gold medals both times. During the 2015 tournament, he scored eight goals and assisted on seven others in seven games. He was named the tournament's most valuable player (MVP).

Matthews was too young to enter the NHL draft after he finished with the national team. He could have gone to college or to the major-junior level. Many other top players did that. But as usual, he took a different path. He went to Europe and played professional hockey in Switzerland for the Zurich Lions.

》》》 Matthews wears a Zurich Lions shirt.

RISING STAR IN SWITZERLAND

Matthews's mom and sister moved to Switzerland with him. Even though he was just 18 years old, Matthews was one of the Lions' best players. He led the team with 24 goals. At the end of the year, he earned the Swiss National League's Rising Star Award and finished second in MVP voting.

Matthews is a center in hockey. Hockey players who are centers have to cover the most ice during a game. Experts saw Matthews's skills as a center. They believed Matthews was ready for the NHL.

Hockey Heritage

Auston Matthews's mother, Ema, is a native of Mexico. That makes Auston one of the few Latino players in the NHL. In 1998, Scott Gomez became the first Latino player to be drafted in the first round and the first Mexican-American to play in the NHL. Gomez played in the NHL for 17 years. Bill Guerin, who played in the NHL from 1991 to 2010, was the NHL's first Latino player. Current Latino players in the NHL include Matt Nieto of the Colorado Avalanche and Max Pacioretty of the Vegas Golden Knights.

>>> Matthews (right) fights for the puck against Matthias Bieber of the Kloten Flyers in 2015.

FACT

Matthews wears jersey number 34, the same that he wore in Switzerland and for some of his U.S. teams. He says he chose it because it was his dad's number as a baseball player.

CHAPTER FOUR

MAPLE LEAF LEGEND

The Toronto Maple Leafs are one of the great teams in NHL history. From 1915 through 1967, they won 13 Stanley Cups. But then the team went without a championship win for a long time. They wanted to draft a star player to lead them to another title.

On June 24, 2016, in Buffalo, New York, the Maple Leafs had the first pick in the NHL draft. The choice was clear. After watching Auston Matthews dominate in every league he played in, Toronto announced they were taking Matthews.

Matthews was nervous until he was drafted. When interviewed that day, Matthews said, "I want to be an impact player. I believe I can be a franchise centerman, a number one centerman in the NHL. That's my ultimate goal."

Matthews after being drafted on June 24, 2016. 〉〉〉

>>> Matthews in the opening faceoff against Arizona Coyotes right wing Shane Doan in 2016

Two months into Matthews's rookie season, the Coyotes came to Toronto. Matthews got to play against his boyhood idol, Shane Doan, for the first time. A couple of weeks later, Toronto traveled to Arizona. Matthews got to play in his hometown for the first time as a pro. He had an assist, and the Leafs won, 4-1.

Matthews didn't stop scoring after his impressive first game. He finished his rookie season with 40 goals. Only Pittsburgh Penguins superstar Sidney Crosby scored more goals that season. Matthews also had 29 assists for 69 points. He won the Calder Memorial Trophy as the NHL's Rookie of the Year.

〉〉〉 Matthews posed with the Calder Memorial Trophy on June 27, 2017.

In his first three NHL seasons, Matthews grew into a true superstar. He scored 111 goals and had 205 points. He was also selected for three All-Star Games. Matthews led the Maple Leafs to the Stanley Cup playoffs each of those seasons. Toronto missed the playoffs three times in a row before that. In 2019, Matthews scored five goals in seven playoff games against the Boston Bruins. The Bruins won the first-round series, and the Leafs' season ended.

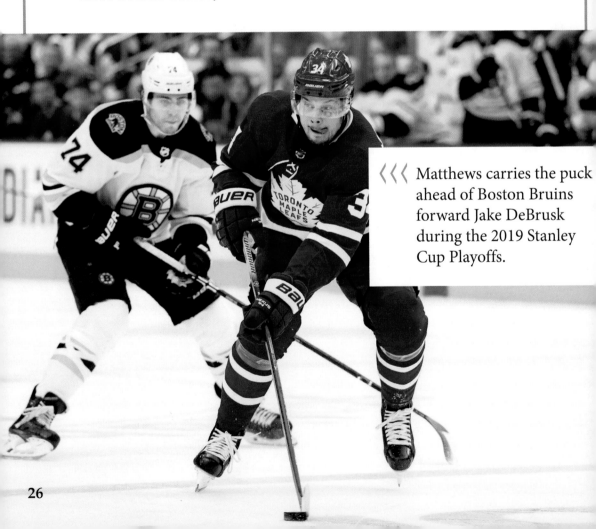

⟨⟨⟨ Matthews carries the puck ahead of Boston Bruins forward Jake DeBrusk during the 2019 Stanley Cup Playoffs.

Auston Helping Out

Auston Matthews was taken to his first NHL game by his dad, Brian, and his uncle, Bill. Bill Matthews died of a disease called cystic fibrosis. After joining the Maple Leafs, Auston decided he wanted to help other people who had cystic fibrosis. He now visits children who have the disease at the SickKids' Cystic Fibrosis Centre in Toronto. Auston has gotten close to the kids. Early in the 2018 season when Auston injured his shoulder, the kids cheered him up by making videos of themselves telling jokes.

FACT

Only seven players born in the United States have been selected number one overall in the NHL draft: Auston Matthews (2016), Patrick Kane (2007), Erik Johnson (2006), Rick DiPietro (2000), Bryan Berard (1995), Mike Modano (1988), and Brian Lawton (1983).

LOOKING AHEAD

Auston Matthews's journey has taken him to hockey rinks around the world. He's been a star player at every stop, and he keeps getting better. He came from the southwestern United States, but he's now playing in Canada's largest city where hockey is the favorite sport. The hope in Toronto is that he will be the one who helps the Maple Leafs finally win another championship.

〉〉〉 Matthews greets a child outside the Maple Leafs' dressing room.

TIMELINE

1997 Born in San Ramon, California

2012 Joins Arizona Bobcats AAA program

2013 Joins USA Hockey's National Team Development Program

2014 Plays in first World Junior Championships

Plays in first Under-18 World Championships; helps U.S. win gold medal

2015 Turns pro; joins Zurich Lions in Switzerland

Plays in second World Junior Championships; helps U.S. win bronze medal

Named MVP of Under-18 World Championships; helps U.S. win gold medal

2016 Picked number one by Toronto Maple Leafs in NHL draft

Plays in World Cup of Hockey for Team North America

Makes NHL debut, scoring four goals

2017 Plays in first NHL All-Star Game

Wins Calder Memorial Trophy as NHL Rookie of the Year

2019 Signs five-year, $58.17 million contract with Maple Leafs

GLOSSARY

ASSIST (uh-SIST)—in hockey, a pass that leads to a goal; up to two assists can be awarded on any goal

BACKHANDED (BAK-han-ded)—using the back side of a hockey stick blade to shoot the puck

CYSTIC FIBROSIS (SIS-tik fy-BRO-sis)—a disease that affects the lungs and makes breathing difficult

DEBUT (DAY-byoo)—a person's first time doing something

DRAFT (DRAFT)—an event in which professional teams select new players

HAT TRICK (HAT TRIK)—when a player scores three goals in one game

ROOKIE (RUK-ee)—a player in his or her first year

STATISTIC (stuh-TISS-tik)—numbers that describe different things that happen in a game or a season

UNIQUE (yoo-NEEK)—unlike any other

READ MORE

Frederick, Shane. *Pro Hockey Records: A Guide for Every Fan.* North Mankato, MN.: Capstone, 2019.

Kortemeier, Todd. *Auston Matthews: Hockey Star.* Lake Elmo, MN: Focus Readers, 2020.

Scer, Jon. *Top 10 Hockey Heroes.* North Mankato, MN.: Child's World Inc., 2018.

INTERNET SITES

NHL
www.nhl.com

Hockey Reference: NHL Stats and History
www.hockey-reference.com

USA Hockey
www.usahockey.com

INDEX